TERROR IN THE SKIES

A NOVELLA BY ALANA TERRY

ALANA TERRY

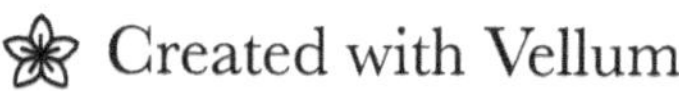 Created with Vellum

ONE

IF YOU WERE to look at me in passing and see my bright blue hair, you might guess I was some kind of art major with a decided bleeding-heart complex. Well, you'd actually be pretty close. Except instead of art, it's theater.

My name is Willow Winters, which if you had any reservations before about my slightly bohemian tendencies, you can assure yourself that your first impression wasn't mistaken. With me it's what you see is what you get. Promise.

It's kind of funny, really. I'm an only child, and so you'd think I'd be more used to being the center of attention, except I'm not. If I had friends who were of marrying age or inclination at this stage in my life, I'd definitely be the *twice a bridesmaid* type or however that saying goes. In fact, even in my theater roles I'm almost always thrown into a critically important albeit nevertheless supporting part.

Fine by me. Fewer people to let down if you mess anything up.

I'm just the blue-haired second fiddle. That could be the name of my autobiography, I swear. Except now I'm stepping into the spotlight. Because it's time for me to tell my own story. My own way.

Are you ready?

Let's go.

It's so funny. Until I moved out here to the East Coast, I didn't think that being from Alaska was any different than being from, oh, say Montana or Georgia or any of the other forty-nine states in the union. But people kind of geek out here when I tell them where I'm from, so I guess I'll go ahead and start there.

Yes, I'm from Alaska. No, I don't ski cross-country to travel from one town to another, nor have I ever seen or spent the night in an igloo. I live an hour away from the nearest grocery store, and my town only has about three hundred people living in it. (Drop that down to a hundred and fifty in the winters if you count the snowbirds.)

Because I'm from Alaska, I'm going to say a few things differently than you. When I talk about going outside, I'm talking about leaving the wonderful beauty of Alaska and venturing out to the Lower 48. (That's the contiguous United States if you're not familiar with the phrase.) A snow machine is what everyone else in the States insists on calling a snowmobile, and breakup season has nothing to do with romantic relationships and everything to do with melted ice and snow.

Because I'm an Alaskan, I'm more than comfortable processing a moose (even though I'm most decidedly vegan), snowshoeing for five or ten miles a day, and using an outhouse. No, I don't drive a team of sled dogs around (although my nearest neighbors do). Yes, I have running water at home (although we have to haul it in on the back of my dad's truck). Yes, I've seen the northern lights, made fireweed jelly, and driven over potholes big enough to drown a beluga.

So, now that we've gotten those preliminaries out of the way, it's time for me to tell you about my most recent trip back home. It's time for me to tell you about the closest I've ever come to dying, and how that experience ultimately saved my life.

TWO

I never had siblings growing up (yes, I know I mentioned that before, but bear with me). Mom and Dad were already fairly old by the time I came around. Having both come from academic lifestyles in the past, they were ready to retire rural, and they brought me along for the ride.

I didn't feel lonely growing up. We had goats, sheep, several dozen chickens, and acres of woods to explore. There was never a shortage of things to do, since my parents were one-hundred percent devoted to subsistence living. By that I mean summers were spent growing all the food we'd need for the winter; falls were filled with canning, blanching, and freezing; and if we couldn't buy or make or grow it local, we learned to do without.

Books were the only exception, and after years of conscience wrangling, my dad even bought himself an e-reader when I was in high school.

Life was simple. Organic. Predictable.

And then I moved to the East for college. It wasn't a surprise, really. Even though nobody from my hometown had ever been accepted to a school like Harvard before, it was tacitly understood I'd be heading toward the Ivy League. My summers spent at camps and enrichment programs all across the country were meant to broaden my horizons and puff up my resumé. Harvard was happy to have me, and as excited as I was to taste the freedom of city living, Alaska has always been and always will be home.

Don't get me wrong. College is fine. I like my classes, I have some awesome friends in the theater department, and I've been cast in quite a few interesting productions already. I've got a great roommate, if you can handle living with a neat-freak bookworm. Seriously, though, Kennedy's amazing. It's kind of an unlikely friendship if you ask me, and since she's going to end up playing a decent part in my near-death experience, I suppose you should get used to hearing about her now.

Kennedy's one of those people you just don't forget. If I'm second fiddle, she's sitting pretty in first chair. Super smart, studious, classic type-A personality. It's a small wonder we shared a dorm room our first year of college without killing each other. But that's just what we did, and we managed to not kill each other with such alarming talent that we decided to go ahead and do the same thing all over again for our sophomore year.

Which brings me to the present.

Or actually to about three months ago.

Winter break.

Kennedy, my oh-so-studious roommate, was coming home with me for the semester holiday. Meet the family. Learn to milk goats, all that fun stuff. Kennedy's a typical city girl, so I thought it would be a blast to offer her that very first taste of rural living.

Fast-forward to day one of winter break. Kennedy had been studying herself sleepless (like normal) to get through all her finals. As for me, two of my classes just had final projects. The others were papers, not all that different than the ones I'd been writing all semester. So basically, Kennedy and I had both made it through another term. It's just that I managed to do it without aging myself a decade and losing a cumulative total of three days of sleep in the process. But that's neither here nor there.

Our first flight to get home was going to take us from Boston to Detroit. Fairly standard, I suppose, as far as airplane trips go. From Detroit on to Seattle, Seattle to Anchorage ... Yeah, getting anywhere when you're from Alaska is a royal pain. Not to mention the fact that even once we landed in Anchorage, we'd still have a five-hour drive ahead of us to get home to Copper Lake. Kennedy's a pretty seasoned traveler. City girl, like I said, all that jazz. Between the two of us, we've probably circumnavigated the world a good number of times if you were to throw our miles together. All that is to say that neither of us was green when it came to flying.

Which is why neither of us had any clue when we boarded that plane how close we were about to come to death.

THREE

HAVE you ever seen someone die before? I know, I know. Morbid question. Too disturbing. I grew up on a farm. I already told you that. So you can guess that I'm not too squeamish when it comes to blood, birth, the circle of life, all that jazz.

Except I'd never seen a human die. Not until I got on that flight with Kennedy.

I'd certainly never seen anyone murdered. But I'm getting ahead of myself.

Let's see … This is the first time I've tried to lay out any of the things that happened to me in any kind of logical order. It's a lot harder than I imagined. I guess I should just start at the beginning.

Kennedy and I were seated in the back

of the plane. I mean the very back. And a few weird things happened right at the start. Well, maybe not totally weird as far as traveling goes, but looking back, they all added up.

So first of all, this Mennonite family got on board. You wouldn't know it if you've never lived here, but Alaska has quite a lot of Mennonites, especially when you get toward Palmer and Wasilla. Most people know the area because that's where Sarah Palin's from. You've heard of her maybe? Fun fact: Jewel is also from Alaska, but that's a less well-known piece of trivia unless you're one of her fans.

So anyway, this Mennonite family came on board. Nothing all that surprising about that, at least to me. If I remember right, this guy in front of me had some kind of problem with them. Made a joke about the Amish not being allowed to fly in airplanes, something ignorant like that. Sadly, not too different than what you might expect.

They seemed like a really nice family too. Quiet kids. Mom was reading to the younger ones if I remember right. But then these two men with Middle Eastern clothing and features came on board. They were sitting toward the front of the plane, but I watched the Mennonite husband and wife exchange a look. I don't have to describe it to you exactly, do I? You know what I mean don't you?

The look.

And then the wife told her husband she had a bad feeling about the flight, and she wanted to get off. I was expecting him to tell her everything was fine. Maybe she hadn't flown much in the past and got nervous. Maybe she'd just watched a documentary recently on 9-11 and hadn't read the memo that not all people of Middle Eastern descent are terrorists. Who knows?

But instead of calming his wife down, the husband called over the flight attendant. Her name was Tracy. Now, think about how many flights you've been on. Not just this year or this decade even, but over your whole life. On a single one of them, can you remember any of the flight attendants' names?

I didn't think so.

But Tracy is a woman I will never forget. Never.

Except I'm getting ahead of myself again. First we need to go back to the Mennonites.

The husband told Tracy he and his wife were uncomfortable and wanted to get their family off the plane. At this point, I expected Tracy to say something like, "Oh, we're perfectly safe here, you have nothing to worry about. Is this your first time flying with us?" If we were ten or fifteen years in the past, she'd probably have offered to give all the kids little wing pins. You remember those, don't you?

Well, that's not what Tracy said. She was very polite and very professional and told them that if they wanted to get off the plane, that was totally their right. So of course that obnoxious man in front of me started complaining about delays, but it happened very quickly and smoothly. One minute they were on the plane. The next minute they were off.

At the time, I'll go ahead and admit it, I thought it had everything to do with racism and xenophobia and that Mennonite woman not wanting to be on a plane with two dark-skinned men wearing turbans. Looking back, I wonder if it was God's way of warning them. I think about that family sometimes. Think about those kids. Did their parents tell them what almost happened?

And what about the parents? Do they feel survivor's guilt? Or maybe some sort of arrogant smugness that they had the good sense to get off that plane? I'll probably never know, but that doesn't mean I don't wonder.

There's a lot of things I wonder about the other victims on that flight. Like Tracy. What did she think about helping that family deboard the plane? Did she think they were being paranoid? Did she begrudge them the extra few minutes of time it took to get them and their luggage back to the terminal? Was she thinking about the paperwork she'd have to fill out to explain the change in the passenger list?

Or maybe she wasn't thinking about them at all. Maybe she was thinking about her two children back home. Or where she'd spend the night once we landed in Detroit. I've read everything I could find about Tracy online, but it still doesn't give a good sense of who she really was. But I think about her escorting that family off the flight. Wonder if she herself had any sort of inkling. Any sort of intuition.

What does a flight attendant do when

they don't feel safe on a flight? They still have to do their job, right?

Which is exactly what Tracy did. Exactly what she'd still be doing right now in fact if things hadn't taken such a terrible, terrifying turn.

FOUR

So I'm going to come right out and say it. I met a guy on the plane. Nothing serious. Nothing that would've led to anything. But I guess now's just a good a time as any to explain to you where I was spiritually when I boarded that plane.

Which was dead.

Spiritually dead, I mean.

My roommate Kennedy was really the first Christian I'd met who wasn't entirely mean-spirited, hypocritical, and judgmental. In fact, her faith made a really positive impression on me. Not that I was looking for a new religion to try on. I was quite comfortable at the time with my blend of agnostic spiritualism with a few borrowings from

Eastern thought, meditation, enlightenment, all that jazz. I was adamantly against organized religion, and other than that I was quite happy to live and let live.

Kennedy was the best kind of Christian friend to have because she wasn't ever shoving her beliefs down my throat. I'd come home on the weekends drunk or high or whatever, and she wouldn't give me a sermon. I asked her about it later, and she said her dad always told her it was wrong to expect non-Christians to act like Christians, which is smart advice if you ask me.

Anyway, back to the flight and this guy I met. He was a teacher. Math, if I remember right, and we got to flirting. We even did a little chair hopping. Kennedy moved over so he and I could sit together. It was really nice of her, now that I think about it, and kind of rude of me. But anyway, I spent a while talking to Mr. Math Babe (not that he was a total babe; I just forget his name at the moment). Which goes to show you what I said before, that this was a typical flight. We were all doing our thing, waiting to eventually land in Detroit. When you think of how much traveling Kennedy and I still had to do to get all the way out to Copper Lake, we'd really just started our trip.

And things were pretty uneventful for the first couple hours. Math Dude was making jokes. Suggesting we get some drinks during my layover in Detroit. The guy in front of us continued to be rude and obnoxious. Kennedy struck up a conversation with this old white-haired retired missionary lady ... It was about as typical as flights get, if not a little chattier than normal.

And then I saw something.

No, it wasn't the two Middle-Easterners. But wouldn't that be a fine setback for the case against racial profiling? It was this big guy in a Hawaiian shirt sitting toward the front of the cabin. Now that I think about it, I couldn't even tell you what it was about him that got my attention. I'm a people-watcher, I guess. Comes from all my time in the theater. Studying people's quirks, memorizing their body language, all that jazz. But there was something about this guy that made me uneasy right from the start.

Maybe it was that gaudy Hawaiian shirt, but there was more to it than that. He was on the flight with this teen girl. I suppose if you were to glance at them real quickly you would have assumed it was a dad traveling with his daughter. And hey, it wasn't too long since I was that age myself. I totally get not wanting to buddy up to your old man, especially in public.

But this was different.

When I looked at them together, I sort of knew they weren't the right fit. Has that ever happened to you? Like once my dad totally embarrassed everybody involved when he starting chatting it up with this middle-aged man at the Anchorage theater. And yes, striking up a conversation with a complete stranger is totally something my dad would do. As would assuming that the young, pretty woman sitting beside him was his daughter and not only making that assumption but saying so out loud.

Hello?

They were obviously a couple, and I knew that from the start, but I couldn't explain to you how I figured it out right away and good old Dad didn't. Well, it was the same thing on the plane. I looked at that middle-aged, balding man, looked at the teen girl he was traveling with, and I knew they weren't right. I kept watching them, kept trying to figure out what it was about the way they were sitting together that creeped me out.

Knowing what I know now, I almost wish I'd said something sooner. But who could tell if that would have helped? Anyway, I kept watching this couple that certainly wasn't a romantic couple and almost certainly wasn't related if I were to trust my instincts. But what was I supposed to do? Just walk up to the flight attendant and tell her that some old guy on the plane was weirding me out?

So I was keeping half of my attention on those two and half of my attention on my roommate. Mr. Math Babe had moved back to his old seat to work on grading papers or something, so it was just Kennedy and me. Talking about what?

They say that when you're in the midst of intense danger, your brain focuses in on the smallest, sometimes most random details. A kind of protective measure so that you can avoid that particular danger again, I suppose. Honestly, you'd have to ask my roommate about that. She's the science nerd. But you'd think, given everything that was about to happen, my conversation then with

Kennedy would somehow be forever seared into my memory.

Except it isn't.

I'd like to think that we had some heavy, weighty discussion about God, the afterlife, anything. But like I said, Kennedy and I didn't usually talk religion. At all. She's quiet. Unassuming in her I'm-going-to-study-until-three-o'clock-in-the-morning-and-ace-all-my-tests overachieving kind of way.

My best guess? We were talking about things like how excited I was for Kaladi Brothers coffee once I landed back in Alaska and whether or not I thought I'd take Math Babe up on his offer for drinks at the airport.

Sometimes I hate how frivolous I can be. I mean, if I'd had any idea what was about to happen, if I had any clue how close I'd come that day to spending an eternity in hell … Sometimes I want to grab Kennedy by the shoulders and shake her and demand, "Why didn't you tell me sooner?" Except now that I'm a Christian myself, I totally get it. It's not like you get saved and all of a sudden have this unavoidable urge to convert the whole world. Or maybe you even have the inklings of an urge, but you talk yourself out of it. *I don't want to scare him away. I don't want her to think I'm judging her. I don't want them to assume I'm some kind of closed-minded, religious nut-job weirdo.*

I get it. I really do. But it's sobering, too. Because back when I was convinced I was going to die, I was scared out of my mind. Scared that maybe I wasn't good enough for heaven after all. It's only by the grace of God I'm alive today. Except now I'm going to remember the lessons I learned on that flight. I'm not going to take my days for granted anymore. I'm not going to be so flightly (no pun intended) that all I care about is getting drinks with some cute math teacher.

And I'm going to thank God every day that he forgave me for my sins and saved me from an eternity of fire and terror. Because I've tasted enough fire and terror on earth. I certainly don't want it chasing me into the afterlife.

I'm saved now. And I thank God for that. But it's terrifying to think of how close I came to the end without knowing him at all.

How close I came to dying with no hope or chance of salvation whatsoever.

FIVE

While Kennedy and I were wasting our time talking about nothing at all significant, I was still eyeing that big man in the Hawaiian shirt and the teen he was with. At one point, he leaned over and said something to her, and she pulled away. It happened so fast I can't be certain I actually saw it, but I could have sworn he yanked her by the hair.

That's when I finally did tell the flight attendant. Tracy. The one whose name I'll never forget. The one whose family background I've checked online a hundred times to see if there's anything more to learn about her.

Mother of two. The family's trying to

stay out of the public eye (yeah, good luck with that), but one picture from a family vacation has been all over the press. It's Tracy and her kids, out camping in the woods somewhere. She was married too, so I kind of assume her husband was the invisible man behind the camera. And they look so happy. So happy and healthy.

So alive.

I told Tracy that this man pulled that girl's hair back. Mentioned that she looked super uncomfortable with him. I don't know if this is where your mind goes or not, but I immediately started to think human trafficking. It's absolutely ridiculous how many Americans are convinced that sort of stuff doesn't happen in their own backyards. I'm pretty sensitive to it. As a feminist, even as a halfway decent human being, there's no way I can stand for any sort of enforced slavery. It's terrible. And absolutely disgusting if you ask me how many smug suburbanites sit in their comfortable middle-class privilege and assume that any girl — any *child* — who's subjected to rape, violence, and exploitation on an hourly basis must *like* the life she's chosen.

So yeah. You probably don't want to get

me started on that. But that's exactly where my mind went. Strange man flying across state borders with a teen girl who's obviously uncomfortable with him? No, I'm not paranoid to have worried that's what was going on.

I didn't tell Tracy all of my suspicions. You'd be proud of me. I spared her the lecture, the statistics, the stories of trafficked girls I've read online. But I did tell her about how that man pulled her hair and yanked her head back. I was sort of thinking she'd poo-poo it away, but she was actually very professional about the whole thing. "Thanks for bringing this to our attention," and "we'll definitely keep our eyes on them," that sort of thing. It's nice to have your concerns validated.

And then we waited.

Except what we thought we were waiting for was the plane to land in Detroit.

I'm so ashamed to think that after I brought up my observations to Tracy, my biggest concern was whether or not I'd join Math Babe for drinks. We had several hours' layover ahead of us, but I didn't want to ditch Kennedy or make her feel like the third wheel. It's kind of funny since she's the one who not only saved my life that day but also introduced me to the Lord, but at the time, I still felt like I was the one who was looking out for her.

She was real sheltered growing up. At least in some ways. Private all-girls' school. Paranoid, safety-addicted father breathing down her neck. Stay-at-home mom baking cookies every day of the week. That sort of thing. It could have been any upper-class American suburb, except the only difference was it was overseas. You should have seen my face last year when I learned my college roommate grew up as some missionary kid. I was totally convinced she'd be this back-wards, socially incompetent child who wore Catholic school-girl uniforms (and I'm not talking about the Halloween party kind, by the way). So I was pleasantly surprised to discover just how normal Kennedy actually was. If spending five hours a day studying for a test that's still two weeks away can ever be considered normal.

The point I'm trying to make is I felt like it was my job on campus to look out for Kennedy. She had this whole international city chic thing going on, but in other areas she was totally clueless. Like the first time one of my theater friends and I decided to medicinally help ourselves reach a state of deeper relaxation (if you get what I'm saying), Kennedy came back to our room a few hours later and seriously had no idea what the smell was. She asked me if I had put on some new kind of perfume. I should point out that I'm doing my best to give up that sort of thing now that I'm a Christian, but I'm not going to lie or pretend that I didn't come from a pretty hard partying background.

I actually used to pity Kennedy for being so up-tight. Thought it was my job to teach her how to let her hair down (both metaphorically as well as literally). I thought she was sheltered and naïve for her beliefs. And I'll go ahead and admit that I teased her sometimes. It was all in good nature, I should mention. She never got angry. Never fought back. On the other hand, she didn't do what some Christians might have done and made the practicing of her faith that much more obnoxious just to spite me.

No, she kept on living her quiet, Christian life, never realizing how closely I was watching. Never realizing that with each passing week my respect for her grew more and more.

Never guessing that when I came face to face with death on that doomed flight to Detroit, it was the God she served so quietly and steadfastly that I'd call on to come and rescue us both.

SIX

Okay, so this is admittedly a little bit of a sidetrack, but can someone please explain to me why the majority of Christians today seem so against environmental progress? I mean, I see how your faith will impact your politics when it comes to things like abortion. I totally get that.

But seriously? When did conservative Christians decide to leave the environmental debate up to everyone else to fight over? Doesn't God in the very first book of the Bible put humans in charge of taking care of the earth? Hello?

I've only been a Christian for a few weeks now, and I know there's still a ton I need to learn. I also know that my specific political leanings may not line up a hundred percent with the majority of Christians, and that's fine with me. I figure that God's judging me based on how much I actually meant it when I asked him to forgive my sins as opposed to how I'll choose to vote in the next election.

But I'm not off my soap box yet. I just need another minute. (And yes, this totally does tie into my near-death experience on that doomed flight to Detroit. I'll get there.)

Did you know that one of the biggest reasons I never even dreamed of becoming a Christian myself was because I thought I'd have to dye my hair back to its natural brunette and start voting for the other guys? Seriously. That's honestly what I thought Christianity was. That's why I'm saying I'm so glad God doesn't judge me based on which box I check when I go to the polls.

I already told you how upset I get about human trafficking, but now I need to talk for a minute about environmental justice. I took a whole course last semester, and I'm pretty well studied up on it.

Did you know that if you go up to a typical pastor and say, "Hey, do you know what environmental justice is?" you're likely to either get a blank stare or some kind of tirade about how global warming is a hoax? But that has nothing to do with environmental justice.

You want a living example? Take the Flint water supply. There's lead in the pipes and no way to fix it. Apparently, it would cost far less to relocate the entire Flint community than to figure out which pipes are leaking lead and poisoning Flint's children (and adults).

That's bad. I'm pretty sure we can all agree on that no matter where we lie on the political spectrum. Right?

But there's more. This isn't just about clean water. This is about class distinction. Because what are you going to do if you're a professional working in Flint, making a multi six-figure income a year and you find out the water there is poisoning you and your family and nobody's going to do anything to fix it?

You move.

Worst-case scenario? Maybe your house forecloses (because who's going to buy land in Flint?). So your credit score takes a hit. But you've got the money, the resources, and the savings account to start over.

Good-bye, Flint. Hello water supply that isn't going to kill you.

Easy as pie.

Now imagine you're an immigrant single mother. You're working two jobs to put food on the table because your income's just high enough you don't qualify for food stamps and just low enough that you can't afford anything. You've got three kids. Those kids have to eat. The baby needs diapers. Oh, and since you're working all the time, you have to pay for all that baby formula.

The problem? The water you're mixing with your baby's formula will eventually kill her.

So what are your options? Well you can buy bottled water. Except oops. That costs more money than you have, and you're already diluting your formula to make it stretch and worried that your baby's health might suffer as a result. Besides, even if you give her purified water to drink, what happens when she needs to wash her hands or take a bath? She's still soaking in poison through that soft, porous skin of hers.

So maybe you wait for the government to come and fix things. After all, poisoned drinking water certainly should fall under the category of a national emergency. Except the government's uncomfortably silent on the matter. I wonder why that is. Could it be because those with the loudest political voices have already taken their trust funds and their retirement accounts and moved away?

Back to choices then. Because after all, this is America. The land of freedom. You have the right to live anywhere you want. Don't need permission to move to a new town.

Except how are you going to afford a moving van? Or a safety deposit on a new apartment? And what about the fact that you're too busy working your two jobs just to keep the kids from starving that you literally can't start over?

And so you stay. And each and every time you fill up that baby's bottle, even though you're using a filter and hoping that will help even just a little, you have to wonder if while nourishing your daughter, you're also killing her.

Slowly. Methodically.

Because this is what happens when you're poor and voiceless and living in the land of the free.

Am I off my soapbox? I suppose for now. But I just had to get that off my chest.

Going back to what happened on that flight, there's absolutely no excuse for murdering innocent victims in cold blood. No reason anyone should stand up and shoot a flight attendant execution style.

Nor is there any reason whatsoever in which it is justified to tamper with a flight carrying hundreds of people. People who are going to die because of your callous decisions.

Sometimes when I wake up from nightmares, the sound of gunshots reverberating in a stark airplane cabin in my ears and the scent of smoke in my nose, I'm tempted to hate the men who did this.

Except I can't.

I can't hate them because — even though I could never justify their actions — I understand exactly why they felt this act of homegrown terrorism was the only solution to their plight.

SEVEN

Before going on, I'd like to apologize to you for my little mini rant back there. Probably wasn't one of my finest moments, I'll be honest. But I've read some of the news articles involving the crash lately, and a lot of people are asking those kinds of questions.

If things were so bad in Detroit, why didn't they just leave?

Why'd they hijack a flight with hundreds of innocent passengers on it when they could have just telephoned their state representative?

I've made myself a promise not to go off on another tirade. Suffice it to say that comments like these really get under my skin. If I were slightly less self-aware, I might even wonder if this was a case of Stockholm syndrome, if I'm sympathizing with the terrorists who nearly killed me for some twisted psychological reason or other.

But I'd been studying what was going on with Brown Elementary School over there in Detroit for months. I already knew which side of the aisle I was on.

Nearly losing my life to a couple desperate, deranged terrorists didn't change that.

Not at all.

But I suppose I'm getting ahead of myself.

It should be Kennedy who tells you about the letter. She was the one who got it, but it completely confirmed every disgusting suspicion I had about that man in the Hawaiian shirt and the girl he was with.

Everything except for the trafficking angle, at least.

I didn't see it happen, but Kennedy got up to use the bathroom. She had to go to the front of the plane because there just so happened to be a man planting a bomb in the lavatories in the back. Of course, none of us knew it at the time. We just thought he'd fallen on the wrong side of an argument with a taco truck on his drive to the airport.

I keep trying to remember what I was

doing when that girl reached out to Kennedy for help. It's not like I thought it was my duty to stare at my roommate as she walked up the aisle just to use the bathroom on an airplane. Truth be told, I was probably wasting time on my phone. Or maybe touching up my makeup since we were now less than an hour away from Detroit, and I was still seriously considering taking a quick detour to go on a date with Math Babe.

I heard the man yell first. And I looked up and saw him shouting at Kennedy. The girl he was with, the teen I'd had my eye on, was terrified. I wouldn't even say she screamed for help. It was more like a squeal. Like something you'd hear from a dying animal.

Everything's a little fuzzy in my mind as I recall it. Maybe because it was so shocking. Or maybe because watching someone yell at your roommate and hearing a terrified teen scream-ing, "Help, I've been kidnapped," isn't as trau-matizing as nearly dying in a fiery plane crash.

But there I go again getting ahead of myself.

The girl was screaming. Kennedy stood there dazed, not that I can blame her. I doubt I'd have had any sense to do anything different. A man in a suit jumped out of his seat in an instant. The air marshal. The hero coming to save the day.

The girl kept shouting, "He's kidnapping me," the air marshal got the Hawaiian shirt dude in handcuffs, and everyone lived happily and safely ever after.

I wish.

Because as it turned out, the main point of the whole scene was to get the air marshal to reveal himself. Couple quick moves — I don't even remember them they were so fast — and the air marshal was knocked out. The guy in the Hawaiian shirt grabbed the officer's gun, gave it to this other man who was in on the entire thing, and we were officially hostages.

There's this type of therapy where you go back and relive traumatizing events, but you do it in this almost dreamlike state where you're in control of the outcome. So you can go back and revisit the moment of terror and give it any ending you want. I haven't been to any actual psychologist or anything, but I've tried this little technique on myself from time to time, and here's my favorite out of all the happy ending scenarios I've come up with.

First of all, who comes to the rescue but Math Babe? (I've started to feel awful I've forgotten his name, so in my imagination I call him Raul.) Raul jumps out of his seat, halfway graded math papers flying everywhere. "Stop!" he shouts in a deep, husky voice. And then there's this fairly exciting but totally one-sided scuffle, the end result of which is both hijackers knocked out and bloody. Passengers cheer. The air marshal wakes from his beauty sleep, his assailants are bound and tied, and we all land safely at the Detroit airport where Raul and I share extravagant tapas and drinks.

End of story.

Pretty good one, isn't it?

I was somewhat proud of it.

But of course, if that's what really happened, I wouldn't have become a Christian. Which leads me to a question I've been wrestling with for weeks. Did God *cause* our plane to get hijacked because he knew that experience is what it would take to wake me up and bring me to my senses? What about the people who died? What about that poor kidnapped girl?

The more I think about it, the more I hate the thought that God wanted the plane to crash just so my soul could be saved. I mean, I'm already dealing with enough survivor's guilt as it is. I'm just going to leave it at I have absolutely no idea. Maybe I'll ask Kennedy's pastor or something. He seems to have all the answers, which is just fine because I'm still so brand new to this whole Christian thing and can't be expected to know it all.

So then. We've covered the somewhat uneventful beginning of the flight. I've told you about Hawaiian Shirt and his partner beating up the air marshal and knocking him out. I've given you my thoughts on the politics that led up to the terrorist attack.

So now I guess it's time to dive into all the details of what happened next.

EIGHT

GENERAL HAD the air marshal's gun. And I
have no idea why he took to calling himself
General, but he did. His name's not what's
important. What mattered is he had the gun.
Which meant from that moment on, he was
the one calling all the shots.

I'll go back to that first minute or two.
It's hard to describe the absolute chaos in
the cabin. Like you could literally feel the
fear and confusion in the air. I think that's
what he was counting on. Because seriously.
Let's do the math. One gun. How many bullets could that be, right? I mean, it wasn't
like it was this big automatic assault rifle or
anything. It was just your ordinary, run of
the mill pistol. What's that, like six bullets?

And how many of us passengers? Several hundred, right? It's not like he could have killed us all.

But what do you do when someone starts yelling and calling himself General and waving a gun around in a crowded airplane cabin? You freeze up, you turn off your brain except the one tiny fraction of it that's necessary for your survival, and you do whatever he tells you to do.

Which is exactly what we did.

General ordered us to get out our phones. He wanted us recording everything he had to say, his big manifesto. And maybe it doesn't come as a surprise to you after my tirade a little bit earlier, but General was a Detroit dad concerned about his children's safety.

We're back to Michigan and environmental justice. I'm telling you it's a real thing. If someone's willing to execute innocent bystanders and crash an entire airplane, you'd better believe it's a thing.

A very serious thing.

Brown Elementary School. That's where General's kids were enrolled. Detroit's dirty little secret. And by dirty, I mean it in both the literal and nuanced sense of the word.

Dirty because there was lead and arsenic in the soil, which at one point had been a dumping ground for a pharmaceutical tech company. The area was so toxic, grown men on the construction crews were landing in the ER. Now I don't care who you are. I don't care if you hate environmentalists and think that vegans and Greenpeace are minions of the antichrist. But seriously, who would ever be okay with building an elementary school in a hazardous waste zone?

Now obviously I'm not saying that the answer to this debacle would be to kidnap a girl, knock out an air marshal, and take over a plane. That's just lunacy. But the inciting event? The anger and the injustice? I'm all over that.

General took his good old time telling the cameras all about how unfair it was, how the superintendent was to blame, how Detroit had miserably and egregiously let down its children. And you know, if it weren't for the fact that he'd just hijacked our airplane and was waving that gun around, I might have felt more inclined to give him a good old-fashioned *amen* or two.

But obviously none of that goes through your head when you see a crazy man waving a gun around. You're not thinking about those poor kids in Detroit whose health is jeopardized on a daily basis just to save the district a couple extra bucks. You're not feeling the frustration of these parents who are mostly working class, immigrant, and minority families who lack the political clout to stand up for their kids.

No. You're staring at that gun. Wondering what would happen to the cabin pressure if it went off. Wondering if the metal hull of the airplane was built to be bulletproof. Wondering if it would be scarier to die in a plane crash or by gunshot.

Hoping he doesn't notice you. And then when you get your wish, that means you're left to feel both relieved and guilt-ridden for the rest of your life because he's turned his wrath on someone else.

NINE

"WHAT'S YOUR NAME?" the General asked.

"Tracy," she answered. And I wanted more than anything to look away, but I was too scared of the uncertainty. I had to watch.

He asked if she had children. That's how I knew about her two kids even before I saw their family photo in the news.

"Would you like to see your children again?" General asked. Tracy nodded. And in that moment she stopped being a flight attendant. She stopped being an airline employee. This was a woman. A fellow human being. A mother with children she loved, with teeth that rattled, with a voice that cracked as she answered General's questions.

She could have been any of us.

She could have been me.

General wanted to make sure all the cameras were still rolling, that we were all streaming our images and footage to the news-frenzied masses down on solid ground.

Wanted to be sure that everybody knew the exact reason for this woman's death.

"It's the superintendent's fault," he said. "He now has two orphans on his conscience."

And he pulled the trigger.

I don't remember screaming, but I'm sure I must have. Everyone did. Because even though we saw the gun, even though we identified the crazed rage in General's eyes, we couldn't bring ourselves to believe he would actually do it. That he would actually kill an innocent flight attendant.

"You have five more minutes, Mr. Superintendent," General told the cameras. Five minutes until what? Another one of us died?

If you haven't been in a cabin full of terrified passengers and a man bent on terrorizing you all, you might expect me to behave differently. To think differently. I already told you I wasn't a Christian at this point in my life, but I'd lived with one for over a year and kind of knew the basic tenets. Love your neighbors. Pray daily. Ask Jesus to forgive your sins.

And maybe you'll expect me to jump in now and say that's just what I did. Dropped to my knees. Told God I was a sinner. All that jazz.

But while General was waving around his gun and pacing up and down the aisles, I wasn't thinking about God or heaven or my sins or my need of a Savior. Do you know what I was thinking?

That the dead woman lying crumpled in the aisle could have been me.

And that in order to survive, I needed to make myself far more inconspicuous than how I normally appear. For the first time in my life, I cursed my obsession with dying my hair. Who would want to stand out in a situation like this?

But stand out I did. And when General's five-minute timer buzzed, his eyes locked onto mine, and he strode deliberately toward the back of the cabin and stopped right in front of me.

TEN

"Stand up," he told me, and I obeyed because apparently that's what your body does when someone's waving a gun at you. Someone who's just shot and killed another woman not ten feet away from where you are.

I stood up.

"Come here," he told me.

So I did.

"What's your name?"

It's funny because as he was asking me all these questions, I could only think about one thing. *Kennedy will be traumatized if she has to watch me die.* Of course, any and every one of us on that flight were already traumatized. You don't have to personally know the murder victim to feel terrified in a situation like this.

But my mind was on Kennedy. On how goodie-goodie she always was, and look where it got her. On a doomed flight, forced to watch while her blue-haired roommate got executed.

General was still talking to the video cameras. Going on and on about how none of this was his fault, how he didn't want to hurt anybody but this was the only way he could get the people of Detroit to take him seriously.

And I think I prayed. I say I *think* I prayed because it wasn't anything formal. It didn't start with *Dear Jesus* and end with *amen*. In fact, if I had to relive that moment in pristine detail, I'm pretty sure my prayer only consisted of one single word.

Please.

"You don't want to die, do you?" General asked me. I assume I shook my head or gave him some sort of response because he frowned as if he actually felt sorry for me. He let out his breath. "I wish I didn't have to kill you." Somehow as I stared at the tip of his gun pointed straight at me, I had a hard time believing him.

"Your hair's blue," he told me, as if I might not have realized.

"I know."

"You some kind of punk girl?" General asked.

"No." And unless you've had a conversation with a terrorist holding a gun at you with dozens of cameras recording your upcoming execution, you have no right to tell me that hair color is a strange topic of conversation when you're about to literally get blown to hell. To me, it felt just as natural as standing there waiting for death.

"You know those dyes have chemicals in them," he told me.

"I only use all natural." Looking back, I too can see the absurdity of the conversation, but when I mentioned all-natural, he locked eyes with me. And for a second, I saw a man and not my own executioner.

Then the moment passed.

"I'm sorry about what I have to do," he said, except he wasn't talking to me. He was talking to the cameras. The cameras all pointed at me waiting to record my murder.

I hoped my parents weren't watching.

When I relive this event, why I try to get to that state where I can recreate the moment when General decided it was time to pull the trigger, I picture a lot of different plausible scenarios, all of which result in my survival.

Of course there's Math Babe rushing up from behind, tackling my assailant, and saving the day. I'm a self-proclaimed pacifist, but more often than not, this scenario ends with Raul (aka Math Babe) shooting General square in the head. Often I stick around to watch an epilogue, and sometimes it involves a doctor jumping up and declaring Tracy the slain flight attendant was still alive, thank God, and sometimes it involves Raul and me walking hand in hand beneath a gorgeous Detroit sunset after a lovely evening of tapas.

One of my personal favorites is when I stretch out my hand, and with some super skilled ninja moves, I disarm my would-be assailant to the sound of thunderous applause from the rest of the cabin. I never actually kill General in this particular daydream of mine, but I like to remind him that I'd be well within my rights if I did.

We land in Detroit, and an army of hot twenty- and thirty-year-old SWAT men in super tight combat gear showing off each and every one of their well-defined muscles barges in, congratulates me on saving the flight, and holds a celebration on the ground that more often than not involves more tapas.

But it's only in my daydreams where I'm saved by myself, a handsome math teacher whose name is possibly Raul, or a couple dozen SWAT men. The true story is that I was saved by a little old granny lady with a head of white hair and enough courage to put all the heroes of the Bible combined to shame.

ELEVEN

GENERAL HAD JUST APOLOGIZED to the cameras, regretting that he had to shoot me, when this little old lady stood up and told him, "Put that gun down, sonny." And it wasn't so much that she dared to talk back to General, who probably weighed three times as much as she did, but it was the boldness with which she addressed him that seemed to tilt the entire axis of power in the cabin.

General gave a little chuckle, but I could tell by his face he was thrown off. "Who are you?" he demanded, and she smiled at him sweetly and answered, "My name is Lucy Jean, but I insist on being called Grandma Lucy. And I'm here to save this young woman's life."

I'd never been at the wrong end of a handgun before, and I'd certainly never witnessed some ninety-year-old grandma try to talk down a raving terrorist, but sometimes truth really is stranger than fiction.

"If you need a hostage," Grandma Lucy said, her voice as calm and patient as if she'd been discussing the roses in her garden, "why don't you take me instead?"

I hadn't expected General to look even more thrown off than he already did, but his expression at Grandma Lucy's words proved me wrong.

"If you shoot me," Grandma Lucy explained as if she were reciting Bible stories to a class of preschoolers, "you'll still get your point across, and you won't have to worry about murdering someone so young and scared. As for me, I've been ready to see my Jesus for the past fifty years."

She stood squarely between me and the gun, stuck out her chest, and waited.

I'd like to tell you about how I came to my senses, realized how selfish it would be to let this tiny four-foot-tall grandma take a bullet for me, but I was too stunned. I couldn't move. Couldn't think. Couldn't talk.

Surprisingly, Grandma Lucy suffered from none of these problems.

"But before you kill me," she began, "there's something I'd like to tell you. Something your audience might be interested in hearing."

He sneered at her. "Yeah? What's that?" I could tell he was growing impatient.

Grandma Lucy's voice rose in both volume and conviction. "That Jesus Christ is the risen Savior of the world. He is my shepherd, my redeemer, my healer, and my coming king. If you kill me, my soul will leave this broken jar of clay and enter into the presence of God. And since you're doing me such a great honor, I want to return the favor."

What was going on? Was she just stalling? And how in the world was it working? Who was this old white-haired lady? Was she a martyr, some kind of miracle worker, or was she just insane?

And then, believe it or not (did I mention before that truth is stranger than fiction?), this Grandma Lucy lady stretched out her hand, raised it to General's forehead (I'm surprised she could actually reach that high), and she started to pray for him.

After everything happened, once the plane crash-landed and we all got evacuated, I looked for Grandma Lucy. Nobody was supposed to leave triage. Once we got our injuries taken care of, we had to answer all kinds of questions from the authorities.

But nobody knew where Grandma Lucy went.

I'm a little embarrassed to admit it, but I'll just come right out and say it. Sometimes I've wondered if she was really some sort of angel sent to distract General. Because while she was praying and General was focused on her, Raul (remember Math Babe?) and a couple other passengers managed to rush him from behind. I swore to the feds doing the interviews later that I heard the gun go off, but apparently my mind must be filling in blanks because nobody else recalls anything like that, and there were no stray bullets anywhere in the cabin.

Go figure.

It just goes to show that I really can't trust my memory at this point in the story because what I remember most vividly is a gunshot, a whole bunch of screams, and a scuffle that was over before I realized I was still alive. General was subdued. The captain came on and assured us we were just a few minutes away from landing.

The nightmare was over.

That's what we all wanted to believe at least.

But the terror was just beginning.

TWELVE

You ever known one of those people who just always seem to have bad luck? Or maybe now that I'm a Christian I shouldn't attribute it to luck, but I think you probably get what I'm saying. People who have one bad thing happen to them after another until you want to scream to the universe on their behalf, "Haven't they been through enough?"

I've met quite a few people like that in my day. Kennedy's one of them, actually. It seems like at least once a semester she's getting into some kind of terrible trouble or danger. For being the kid of such a safety-paranoid father, she sure has managed to find herself at the wrong place at the wrong time more often than I would care to count.

Well, that's how I'm guessing we all felt on the plane after Raul and a few other brawny passengers managed to get General and his Hawaiian-shirted partner subdued. You'd think by that point, with the hijackers bound and the plane just minutes away from touching down, we could start to let out our breaths. Thank God (or the universe or luck or whatever) that we were safe.

Except we weren't.

Because General and Hawaiian Shirt weren't exactly working alone. And that dude who kept making a nuisance of himself in the back lavatories all through the flight was a Detroit electrician with just enough skill to know how to cause some major damage. This is another case where memories fail, because I'm certain the shouting came first, but others insist it started with the fire alarm going off.

Either way, the back of the cabin was on fire. Smoke began pouring out of the lavatories.

While General had been marching around the cabin with that gun of his, the passengers had remained eerily silent. Now, all that terror we'd been bottling up snapped, and it was complete chaos. I heard later that the paramedics had to treat more people for injuries related to trampling than smoke inhalation.

It was madness. Madness and unceasing terror as everyone raced to the front of the cabin.

I would have joined them. I tried to join them. But someone knocked me down from behind. I have no idea who it was. By this point, the smoke had grown so dense so quickly I could scarcely see anything. I was relying entirely on feel.

And then I stumbled. A woman's high heel stomped on my hand. I cried out, but there was no way to hear anything over the screams of the passengers and the drone of the fire alarm.

Get up, I told myself. *You didn't survive a near-execution just to get yourself trampled to death when you're only a few minutes short of landing. Get up.*

Except I couldn't. There were too many people. Too many bodies. I couldn't stand. Couldn't breathe. Someone stepped on my back. No more air in my lungs. I couldn't even cough out the smoke I'd just inhaled.

And that's when I knew it had happened. My luck had finally run out.

I really was going to die.

THIRTEEN

You ever read any of those stories about people who swear they nearly died and went to heaven? Then they were resuscitated and survived and came back to tell the whole world about their experiences? Apparently Christians are kind of divided when it comes to stories like that. I guess some people think it's all hocus-pocus, maybe even the work of demons (although I really can't understand why a demon would try to convince someone they were in heaven, but that's neither here nor there). Other folks get all into it, write their bestselling books, earn their millions.

I honestly don't know where I fall on that

spectrum. I've already told you that I've only been a Christian for a couple of weeks. Seriously, I'm still trying to figure out what to do with myself on a Friday night now that I'm not allowed to go out and party, so I'm probably not the best person to ask about convoluted matters of faith and theology.

All I can tell you is what happened to me.

And that's basically the reason I'm saved now.

I was stuck. I couldn't move. I don't know if was my injuries from getting stepped on or what. Maybe it was even a literal demon holding me in place, trying to kill me before I had the chance to turn my life around. I seriously don't know.

But I couldn't move. Each time I budged, something caught around my neck. Like something was trying to strangle me.

I was going to die.

And do you know what I thought about? Well it certainly wasn't tapas. Or Mr. Math Babe. Or how terrible Kennedy would feel once I was dead.

I thought about my family. Wondered if they were following the news already or if they were blissfully waiting for their only child to come home, never suspecting the life was seeping out of my pores with every second.

But more than anything? I thought about that little old lady. Grandma Lucy. The one who stood ready to take a bullet for me.

There are people I'd probably die for. My parents, for one thing. Maybe even Kennedy if it ever came right down to it. Underage victims of human trafficking? I'd be willing to risk my life if I knew it would save them.

But this little old lady stood up for me. Told that deranged General she would take my place.

I suppose if you were looking in from the outside, maybe you'd think it made evolutionary sense, in that cold, calculated Darwinian way. Grandma Lucy was old. Had lived her life. Had passed on her genes, blah, blah, blah. And here I was. Young. Healthy. Strong.

So she was willing to trade places.

But there was more to it than that. I wish I could explain to you what I heard in her voice. Wish I could describe the intensity. You ever watch those superhero movies? There's a common trope in a lot of them. This old lady with wicked awesome super-natural powers. The kind who can heal you with a touch or strike fear into villains five times their size.

That's the kind of power I sensed in Grandma Lucy when she stood between me and that gunman. An unmistakable, never before experienced *power*.

I was agnostic basically my entire life, but I always believed in something divine. Something beyond what science can explain or the eye can see. But I'd never experienced it until that moment. And do you know what it was I felt pouring out of Grandma Lucy?

Love.

She loved me.

Not in the way some do-good Mother Theresa-esque kind of saint would feel warm and fuzzy toward all humanity. This was far more personal.

Far more powerful.

Grandma Lucy loved me. Enough to die in my place, even though she didn't know me. Some people look at my dyed hair, my outlandish clothes, and they write me off as some kind of edgy weirdo. Once at the bookstore I even had a mom tell her child, "Don't make eye contact with her." So yeah. I may not be part of a marginalized minority in any real sense of the word, but I certainly have experienced my share of prejudice. Of being written off as "other."

But Grandma Lucy saw past all that. It was like she was seeing the real me.

Me, Willow Winters. A scared young woman who only wanted to get home to her mom and dad.

And she was willing to die in my place.

She'd already saved my life once. I knew that much. I can't recall a single word she said in her prayer while she was staring at that gun, ready to take that bullet meant for me, but I can tell you the power I felt behind her words.

In another culture, another religious era, she might have been called a shaman. A spiritual healer. A miracle worker.

Instead, she was just Grandma Lucy. The most powerful woman I've ever encountered.

Thinking about her gave me hope, and

that's all I had to cling to as I lay on that cabin floor, smoke burning my lungs, stinging my eyes, draining the life out of me. Grandma Lucy loved me enough to save me.

And she hadn't done that so I could die here alone.

FOURTEEN

AT ONE POINT I ended up passing out. Because apparently that's what your body de-
cides to do when you're stuck in a smoke-
filled airplane cabin. You know how I was
talking about near-death experiences, Christians claiming to go to heaven, all that jazz?

None of that happened to me.

But *something* did.

I'd like to say I had a dream because that
puts it into a neat little easy-to-define category that everyone can relate to. I mean,
who hasn't ever had a dream while they're
asleep?

Except I really couldn't call it that. Not
while maintaining any sense of literary in-
tegrity. Imagine a dream that's even more

real than the physical world. Where the moment you're in it everything flips around and you realize that the earth you've always called real is actually the dream and you've never been truly awake until that very moment.

Then imagine that love isn't just some esoteric emotion or a word you use to describe how you feel about your family or your dog or your favorite vegan tapas bar. Imagine that in this real world, the one that makes everything you've ever known seem like the dream, love is an actual, tangible force. And that force is pouring into you, like the most powerful waterfall you could ever imagine, except instead of drowning you, it makes you feel like for the first time in your entire existence you're actually alive.

And part of you doesn't want to wake up and go back to the real world because this power you feel is so tangible, but you also know you're not ready to leave the dream yet. There's more you have to do.

If you can picture all of that, and if you have what could be called the most active imagination out of every human who's ever lived, you might be able to grasp at least the smallest fraction of what I experienced.

And then the feeling was gone. The dream was over.

And all that was left was terror and fear and pain.

And smoke. So much smoke …

FIFTEEN

Between the time I passed out and woke up in the Detroit hospital, I have literally no recollection, and so I'm free to make up whatever turn of events I'd like.

My initial go-to is that once we landed, Raul rushed to the back of the cabin, frantically screaming my name until he found me. He knelt down, swooped me up, and raced me off that plane, shouting, "This woman needs a medic!"

Other days, I kind of like the idea of Grandma Lucy walking off that plane (she's totally fine as I envision the scene in my head because she's got some kind of Holy Spirit bubble surrounding her that kept the smoke out and the oxygenated air in). Once she gets onto the tarmac, she kneels down, thanks God for his protection, and senses with powerfully divine intuition that I'm in trouble. At which point she prays for God to send a couple angels to get me off the flight, and these heavenly beings are quick to comply.

It's also quite possible that my rescue was far more mundane, that the first-responders who were on the scene when we made crashed in Detroit were simply doing their job. Which doesn't make my survival any less miraculous or my saviors any less heroic.

Now, if this were a little Christian novel I was writing, if I were relying on fiction instead of hardcore, actual fact, I'd probably wrap things up with me on my knees in a hospital room, folding my hands together, praising God for his salvation and begging him to forgive my sins. At which point, I'd probably commit my entire life to becoming a missionary in Africa, taking selfies with a bunch of orphans, all that jazz.

Well, I hate to let you down, but I've got to tell things like they are.

Yes, I experienced my first real taste of divine intervention and heavenly power on that flight. No, I will never forget that sense of love that poured into my soul after I passed out.

But that doesn't mean I turned my life around the second I woke up in the hospital. Even now, weeks after my conversion, I really couldn't say my life's been *turned around*. Turns out this whole Christian walk is a lot harder than it looks, and it took me quite a while before I was ready to actually bend the knee to Christ (figuratively, I should say; I never actually got down and knelt, which Kennedy as well as her pastor assure me isn't required for salvation).

The other thing you probably wouldn't expect me to talk about right here is the nightmares I still have about that flight. Sure, I can joke all I want about getting rescued by Math Babe Raul or irresistible SWAT teams in their kick-butt, bullet-proof gear. But more often than not, my dreams are about being stuck in that smoking cabin, realizing I'm not going to make it out alive, knowing that I'm not ready to die.

I guess that just goes to show that even when God swoops down and literally saves you out of the pit of hell, sometimes it still takes a little while before you're ready to acknowledge him.

After our rescue, I spent my entire semester break in Alaska with Kennedy thinking about what happened to us. Asking her questions about what it would mean if I actually were ready to become a Christian. And she wasn't pushy. Wasn't over-zealous to get me to sign on the dotted line. I think she knew I needed to figure all this out in my own time and in my own way.

I was so scared of flying back to campus after all we went through (we were both basket cases on that flight back to campus, truth be told), that I made my first bargain with God. If he gave me that same sense of power and love and protection out on the flight back to campus, I'd spend the upcoming semester studying the Bible and deciding for real if I was ready to get serious about this whole Christianity thing.

Well, there wasn't anything nearly as dramatic as when I'd passed out in the cabin, but I wasn't quite as scared as I expected I'd be either. I guess I can say God met me halfway.

So I did the same for him.

Kennedy and I started doing this Bible study together some nights when we were both in our dorm room and she didn't have her nose buried in her books. I found a couple preachers online I liked and began listening to their podcasts. It was right before Valentine's Day if I remember correctly that I told Kennedy I was ready to go ahead and jump into the Christian life. At the time, I really didn't know what that meant, and to be honest, I'm not sure that even now I do. Like I said, I don't have a clue when it comes to debates about theology or all that jazz. What I do know is that I was saved by God, first physically on that flight and then spiritually just a few weeks ago.

Took me long enough, some believers might say. But I didn't want to jump into something one minute only to decide a few days or weeks later it wasn't going to work out. I knew that if I planned to commit, I needed it to be serious.

Am I serious about my faith now? I think so. Like I said before, I've given up partying, at least the aspects of that lifestyle that are inherently sinful. That's a pretty big deal for someone like me. And I'm studying my Bible with Kennedy. We're praying together too. It's like we're an old married couple saying our bedtime prayers before lights out. Sometimes I feel bad that I wasn't instantaneously turned into Miss Sunday School Goodie-Goodie like Kennedy right away, but I suppose everybody matures differently, right? At least that's the excuse I'm telling myself.

Sometimes, I'm a little embarrassed that it took something so drastic as getting my flight hijacked, witnessing murder, and nearly dying to get me to accept Jesus. I mean, some people hear the gospel once and decide to be saved. And I'll be the first to admit that the survivor's guilt is awful. I may not be the best at praying yet, but I do pray for poor Tracy's family every time I think about her.

Maybe one day I'll look up her two kids and tell them how brave their mom was. How much she loved them. How she didn't want to leave them.

But for now, I'm still covering the basics. Trying to remember to read my Bible each day. It still doesn't make sense how I could have done so many sinful things and I only had to pray once for God to forgive me, so I'm spending a lot of time confessing right now. Just in case I forgot some things the first time.

I think about Kennedy, about how mature she is in her faith. Then I compare that to Grandma Lucy, who I never did manage to find after our plane landed. It can be overwhelming at times, realizing how much I still have to learn. How far I still have to go.

But I guess that's part of the Christian journey. One step at a time. And maybe what matters isn't whether or not you're taking baby steps or giant leaps as long as you're headed in the right direction.

I certainly hope so at least.

My name is Willow Winters. I'm a theater major. Airplane hijacking survivor. Blue-haired second fiddle.

And now, by the grace of God, I'm saved.